bear

Tom Lang (signature)

A Story by
Tom Lang

Published by: BOUDELANG PRESS
                 P.O. Box 3005
                 Venice, CA 90291-9998
                 TEL. 310.712.5606
                 WEB SITE: **www.boudelang.com**
                 E-mail BOUDELANG @aol.com

Illustration and Concept by Andrew Reidenbaugh

Design by Siobhan Burns

Editing by Laurie Insley

Production by Sandy Hubbard

Library of Congress Catalog Card Number pending

ISBN 0-9649742-6-6

I'M A BIG, BAD ALASKAN BROWN BEAR AND I GET A little angry now and then. So shoot me. I don't live in a fairy tale world where the worst thing that can happen is a smelly human eats my porridge and sleeps in my bed. I live in the real world. One day you're walking down a trail smelling the flowers, the next your head's hanging on a cabin wall and the humans are sitting on your butt in front of the fireplace.

My last rampage started late this spring. I was eating salmon, alone as usual, along side the riverbank. A herd of cars stopped and humans got out pointing and staring at me. I moved up river but they followed me, their cameras making little insect noises. After my second salmon I snapped. I dropped the carcass and charged toward the road. The humans screamed as they raced to their cars. I banged on windows and I stood on hoods. I chewed on tires until they exploded.

"Are we having fun yet?" I growled, ripping a funny looking boat off the top of a truck and crushing it with my paws.

For the next few weeks I scared every human I could find. I shadowed campgrounds at dusk, waiting for the humans to go to sleep. Then I banged on their trailers or ripped open their tents. I sniffed along hiking trails, listening for the sound of bells and the weak squeak of the human voice. Humans always fall for the old fake charge technique. I jump out of the bushes, roaring and romping at full speed, then slam on the brakes a few feet in front of them before their smell knocks me into a coma. While the humans lie shaking, curled up in balls, I tear into their backpacks and eat their food.

Is my behavior a bit extreme? Perhaps, but I've been on edge since cubhood. I'm an insomniac. I haven't had a sound winter's sleep since I was two years old. Most brown bears catch some shuteye and hibernate for five or six months. I spend my winters lying in my six-foot-long, four-foot-wide den and staring up at my three-foot-high ceiling. I count blueberries and jumping salmon. I memorize moose anatomy. Nothing works. The few times I slip into slumber I am startled awake by my troubled dreams.

At the peak of my rage this year my brother Ted came up to me as I was sneaking up on one of those humans who run for miles for no apparent reason.

"Hey, bro," he said. "I've been looking for you. Hungry?"

"I'm always hungry, Teddy."

"I have a moose hind quarter that's rotting away and I thought you and me could sit and feast on it."

"Twist my paw."

Although we live in the same valley, my brother and I don't see each other much and we haven't been close since we were cubs. But a free meal is a free meal. I followed him through the woods, making small talk: "…is it just me or are the glaciers melting faster this year… I hear there's a new parasite going around…those damn wolves."

We arrived at a clearing, a grassy moose meadow where twenty bears sat in a circle. The legendary Big Bear stood in the center while the group stared at me. Big Bear beckoned me forward with the curl of a claw. He put his big paw over my hump.

"You know everybody," Big Bear said, his voice thunder from the sky.

The bears grunted and snorted "hellos."

"What's this all about?" I said, glancing over at my brother. Teddy turned away from me and looked down at his back legs.

"This is about you," Big Bear said, first pointing at me then spreading his front legs toward the group, "and this is about us."

I nodded and waited.

"You're causing trouble with the humans," Big Bear said.

The bears in the group grumbled and huffed.

"So? They started it."

"And they'll finish it. Humans began slaughtering our forebears 200 years ago. There were 100 thousand of us down in the lower 48 ranges back then. Now there are only

1,000. We still have 30,000 brown bears in Alaska and we want to keep it that way. Your behavior does no one any good."

"I can't see what difference my behavior—"
Big Bear raised his paw to silence me.

"They come looking for you they come looking for all of us. Humans are stupid. We all look alike to them. They can't smell. Our sense of smell is 75 times stronger. The olfactory mucosa in a human's nose is less than a square inch. Ours is 100 times that. Humans are at the bottom of the evolutionary ladder."

"Exactly, Big Bear, so what's the problem?"

"The problem is this; by stepping down to the human's level, which you are doing by attacking for no reason, you create a problem for all of us. Humans are reactive and irrational. All they need is one lame excuse and they'll start picking us off like berries from a bush."

"What do you expect me to do about it?"

"We expect you to change your behavior. All bears have potential problems with humans. But you have a bigger problem with yourself. You're acting out. It is the summation of the Benevolent Order of Brown Bears of the Chilkat Valley that you visit Dr. Carnivora Chordata, our anger management therapist in residence."

"Or what?" I said, heat rising under my fur.

The group of bears stood up and surrounded me.

"Failure to do so," Big Bear said, squeezing my shoulder, "will give us no other choice but to ban you from the premier spawning grounds, restrict your roaming on Blueberry Hill and revoke your forest toilet privileges until we see fit."

I am walking through the woods on a perfect day, my nose sucking in the sweetness from the air. Spring flowers arch toward the sun, birds play call and respond and little creatures dart in and out of the brush. I whistle a tune while the trees sway back and forth in rhythm. A wolf appears on the trail in front of me.

"Morning, Mr. Bear, you are looking good," the wolf says. "Niiiiiiiice coat."

"Thank you, Mr. Wolf," I say.

I begin to skip along the trail, whistling, loving life. Around the next turn a moose antler hits me in the head.

"Hey, that's a top-of-the-line fur you got there, pal," the moose says.

"Thank you very much, Mr. Moose, only wish I had one of those things you have hanging under your chin."

"Dewlap, Mr. Bear, it's called a dewlap."

"Whatever."

I continue on my way, bouncing and singing. A flutter of wings gives my tune a backbeat. I look up at a bald eagle circling above the tree line.

"I thought I had beautiful feathers, but you've got one nice set of duds there, Mr. Bear."

"Thank you, Mr. Eagle," I say, saluting him with my right paw. As I step into a creek a school of sockeye salmon jumps into the air.

"Wow," the pool of voices scream, "look at the beautiful coat, fit for the king of the forest, which you are, of course. All hail Mr. Bear!"

"Thank you little buddies."

I stop midstream, pinched by my instincts. The forest is silent, earthquake quiet. I look around. The wolf, moose and eagle are staring at me, smiling. The salmon are huddled in an eddy, giggling. A streak of cold shakes me as I look down at my paws. They're hairless. I check my legs, chest, hump. I have no coat at all, naked as a newborn cub.

"Now, there's a bare bear," the wolf says, howling at his own joke.

The moose laughs so hard he falls down, clapping his hooves together. The eagle flaps his wings, an owl hoots from the trees, the salmon jump in and out of the water slapping their fins. The forest shakes with laughter.

I run through the woods, smashing into trees and trampling plants and flowers. I hide behind a large rock, hugging myself as I shiver in the cold, the cackles and snickers thundering in my head.

"HOW DID YOU FEEL WHEN YOUR MOTHER ... UM ... separated from you?"

"You mean abandoned me?"

"Okay, abandoned you. How did you feel?"

"How would you feel?"

"We're not here to talk about me, Mr. Brown."

I stood up. The sweet aroma of a distant dead moose filled me with cubhood memories of hunger and loss. I stared off into the mountains above Dr. Chordata's office.

"How old were you when your mother left?"

"Left, ha!" I huffed as I paced back and forth. "Kicked us out and ran off with a new guy. We were only two-and-a-half years old. We were little cubs, barely 200 pounds."

"Eighty percent of mothers separate from their children at the start of the third summer," Dr. Chordata said, smoothing her coat with her claws.

"And that makes it right?"

I crushed an elderberry bush as I stomped to my left.

"Mr. Brown, you know the rules: no roaming. Please lay back on the skunk cabbage."

I puffed out a breath and dropped to the ground into the large leaves of the plant.

"When your mother…went away…did you talk to her?"

"Of course I did. I begged Mama not to go?"

"And what did she say?"

"She grunted that I was ready. Ready!"

"Uh-huh."

"I tried to reason with her but she told me to stop whining. Then she hushed me, said she sensed trouble and told my brother and me to climb a tree. I told her we were brown bears, not black bears, and that black bears climbed trees, not brownies like us. She told me to quit being smart, slapped us on our behinds and told us to hide in the bushes. Then she ran off."

My breathing was labored, moisture was clouding my eyes, a marmot was stuck in my throat.

"And?" Dr. Chordata urged.

"We hid in the bushes for days waiting for her. It was cold and we were hungry and we could hear the wolves howling all night long."

"Go on."

I sat up shaking, my mouth dry, all 42 of my teeth grinding together. A cub-like sound, the hoarse bark of a fox, coughed out of my mouth.

"She never came back…"

Dr. Chordata leaned forward.

"Then what did you do?"

"With our noses to the ground we searched for days for her. We found her in a meadow flirting with a huge male who looked like he weighed ten thousand pounds. They were wrestling with their forelegs. He was biting my mom on her face and her neck and her shoulders. She was biting back, laughing. Then he…he…"

"Then he what?"

I stood up, tilted my head back and roared.

"I think that's enough for today, Mr. Brown."

I AM INSIDE THE BEAR PLUG INN, A BROWN BEAR BAR burrowed out of basalt near the border of the borough. A sign behind the bar reads:

PROUDLY POURING PURE BEAR'S MILK
GUARANTEED 30 PERCENT FAT CONTENT

My brother Teddy is bartending, serving frothy buckets of bear milk while he chugs a mug or two for himself. Big Bear is holding court at the end of the bar, telling stories to the crowd.

17

"So Bobby Bear asked me the most unusual place I've mated and I said, 'That would have to be up the bay, Bob,' when I ..."

Big Bear notices me and stops his story. The bar goes silent.

"What did I tell you about coming in here, kid?" he says.

"C'mon, B.B., just a little taste, one for the trail," I beg through slurred words.

"You've had enough mamas' milk, kid, go sleep it off."

"I can't sleep, I need a drink," I say, heating up.

"You're barred from this bar, Brownie," Big Bear says. "Beat it."

Powerful paws grab me from behind and drag me out of the bar. I look up to see my mother as she dumps me in the gravel. She dusts off her paws, then walks back into the bar. I curl up, shaking. I feel the eyes of a thousand wolves watching me from the forest.

"I SENSE YOU CARRY A LOT OF ANGER TOWARD YOUR mother."

"Wow, Doc, you're smarter than the average bear."

"Sarcasm is often a defense against pain."

"I'm not in pain, I'm just angry."

"I wonder if some of this anger is misdirected."

"Misdirected? A defense against pain? If I had a mother who had done her job I wouldn't be sitting here today."

"The infant mortality rate is thirty-five per-cent in the first year, Mr. Brown."

"Your point?" I said, resting the back of my head on my paws, staring up at the passing clouds.

"Didn't she feed and protect you?"

"By scaring us to death?"

"Scaring you? Tell me more about that."

"Always telling us about the predictions of that crazy 15th century French bear."

"Nostrafursus?"

"Once upon a time, she would say, a bear could safely walk through the woods, but then, just like Nostrafursus said, the death squads came, with coats like trees and bush-es, stalking bears, murdering us as if we were creatures of no significance. All male bears are to blame for the death squads, Mama said. She also told us the crazy Frog bear predicted that young male bears that disobey their mothers would be abducted in the middle of hibernation, made to dance for our food before our gall bladders were cut out and shipped to faraway lands."

Dr. Chordata sat quietly for a moment.

"Is your mother still alive?"

"Oh, yes."

"When did you last see her?"

"Ten years ago."

"So you're 12½ now … you haven't seen her since she left?"

"Correct."

"How do you know she's still alive?"

"I can smell her a mile away."

*I AM WALKING IN THE FOREST AND THE SMELL OF
honey draws me to a cabin. The sweet aroma
is intoxicating; I sway to and fro on my back
legs like I've seen humans do with their bot-
tles around the campfire at night. I shatter the
cabin door. Humans scream as they dive
through windows and curl up in balls. My
paws stick to the floor as I move around, ripping open cupboards, overturning tables.
Honey is oozing down the walls, flooding the*

floors. I'm in heaven. The more honey I eat the more pours from the cabin.

A female scent tickles my nose. Driven by urges I start down a hallway the length of an ice field. In the distance a bevy of sexy female bears lay under a giant cottonwood tree, snacking on a rack of moose. They wink at me, enticing me forward with their foreclaws.

Yes! I run for them but I'm in slow motion, my legs stuck in the honey. The harder I try the deeper I sink. A long legged blondish bear runs her tongue along her teeth while a female with a reddish coat scratches her claws along the branch, leaving a groove in the bark. I'm sinking deeper, the honey up to my chest, thick against my belly, matting my fur. The females frown at me, begin to pout. I call to them but the honey is pouring into my mouth, gagging me. Don't go I say, but I'm drowning in the honey. They turn away from me and gnaw on the moose bones.

"TODAY I WOULD LIKE TO TALK ABOUT YOUR RELA-
tionships with the opposite sex."

I fidgeted in the grass. A ground squirrel
raced by and I snatched it and bit off its head
and offered the body to Dr. Chordata.

"No, thank you. You are almost 13 and
you are still a … well, you haven't mated yet."

I shrugged, looked down at the patch of
purple lupine between my feet.

"A male bear is ready to breed by the

age of five."

"Thanks for reminding me, Doc," I said as I absent-mindedly began digging a hole in front of me.

"I notice you're digging again, Mr. Brown. Remember our agreement on digging? You destroy my office floor every week."

I paused and caught my breath. I had dug five feet beneath the ground. I popped my head up and shoved dirt out of the way. "I'm depressed."

"Uh-huh. Let's talk about your weekend. How was your date with Cinnamon?"

I snorted, kicked dirt back in the hole.

"You two did go out again, yes?"

"Yeah."

"And what happened on your date?"

"Dinner."

"Good. Tell me more about that."

"I took her to the new outdoor restaurant at 10-mile with the salmon spawning stream running through the joint. We both had the rotting-log-stuffed-with-insects special."

"Yum."

"After dinner we swam across the Chilkat to the flats and walked along and talked. Next thing I know she's tripped me with her fore leg and she's biting me on my neck."

"Uh, huh, oh, my," my therapist said, fanning herself with a paw.

"Then we wrestled, bit each other some more…" I said, my voice trailing off.

"Aaaaaand?"

"Nothing. I got upset, knocked down a stand of alder trees. It was her fault."

"Her fault? She wasn't ready? The female sometimes waits four or five dates before mating."

"Oh, she was ready, all right."

"Uh-huh."

I stared down in silence, swatting away a swarm of mosquitoes. Suddenly I jumped into the hole and dug furiously.

"Work on anger, Mr. Brown, let's work on anger."

EVERY TIME SHE SWAYS HER LITTLE TAIL AT ME
It brings out the male in me
I'm in love with the bear next door

I am on stage at the Chilkat Valley Center
of the Ursine Arts. I am dressed in black tie and
tuxedo, a bowler cocked to one side, my paws
spread open, singing to the sold-out crowd.

When we're dancing claw to claw
Ooooooh, there oughta be a law
I'm in love with the bear next door

Cinnamon enters stage left. Her eyes sparkle in the center of her classically beautiful dish-shaped face. Her reddish-brown coat shimmers like a sunset. The audience roars as she breaks into song:

> *Until he tells me I'm his mate*
> *I will wait and hibernate*
> *I'm in love with the bear next door*

Paw to paw, claws entwined, we dance back and forth across the stage, spinning and twirling, the crowd on its back legs clapping its forelegs together. I dip her low to the stage floor, holding one paw while she extends her other to the audience and sings:

> *My head screams out 'beware!'*
> *But my heart just doesn't care*
> *I'm in love with the bear next door*

The next verse is mine but when I try to sing nothing comes out. I'm confused, sweating, afraid. My throat is dry. Cinnamon, always the professional, mouths my next line but I can't hear. I feel the tension in the theater as the crowd huffs and puffs. I watch in slow motion as a salmon carcass flies through the air and lands on the stage in front of me. Then another salmon. The lower leg of a moose hits me on the head, a paw full of blueberries splatter in my face. Now the theater is raining on me. Fish skeletons, Devil's Club bushes, soapberries, old backpacks fly onto the stage. Humiliated, Cinnamon runs off the stage.

DR. CHORDATA COULD BE AS IRRITATING AS A MILE-long tapeworm, but maybe she was right on one point: my anger was a large beaver dam blocking the flow of my life. Huff ten times before I react, she told me. Be aware of situations that trigger my anger. Take control of my life.

The mating season was closing and soon my urges would turn exclusively to food and to bulking up for the winter. Now was my last chance to consummate my relationship with Cinnamon. In the morning I brushed the thorns and nettles from my coat and rubbed salmon oil on my face and neck. Visualize, think positive, make affirmations, Dr. Chordata had told me. Standing on the riverbank I stared at my reflection in the water. *Who's the bear? I'm the bear!*

I swam across the river, heading toward Cinnamon's range on the other side of the valley. I walked through the alder and willow brush, the color of the leaves softening as fall approached. I swam a few more channels until I reached the flats. I came out of the freezing water invigorated. I was confident and strong and ready. *Who's the bear? I'm the bear!*

Cinnamon was facing away from me, eating a salmon. Her sensual behind beckoned to me as I snuck up on her. I gnawed at her back leg. She puffed a few breaths as she turned toward me. She jumped back.

"Oh, hi, Brownie," she said, looking around.

"Hi, Cinnamon, you act surprised," I laughed, my stomach tightening. I noticed her fur was rumpled. I tried to nip at her neck but she pushed me away.

"We need to talk," Cinnamon said.

"I'm ready now, honey. Let's talk later."

"I think it's time we see other bears," Cinnamon said. A familiar feeling of emptiness ran through me. A shiver of ice descended through my body.

"I don't want to see other bears," I said.

She looked at me, her silence stronger than words. I moved toward her again but she held up her paws.

"Please, Brownie, don't make this any more difficult. This relationship isn't working out for both of us and…"

"Things have changed, Cinnamon, I'm a new bear."

"…and you're scaring me," she said.

I heard steps in the gravel. I looked up to my left and a big bear walked toward Cinnamon with a salmon in his mouth. He didn't notice me as he dropped the fish in front of her.

"Hey, honey, here's another salmon for my little salmonberry," he said.

"My little salmonberry?" I said, bees starting to buzz in my head.

"Who's this?" I said, my heart rate rising.

"A…a friend," Cinnamon said.

I took a step toward the bear.

"You got a name…friend?" I said, loosening my neck and shoulders.

"I got a name," he replied, standing on his back legs and sniffing the air around me. "Smells like you've got a problem."

"I'm a problem solver," I said as I hooked him in the head with my left paw. As he stumbled I dug my teeth into his shoulder, ripped out a piece of fur and pushed him into the river. He stood up, put his paw to his shoulder and looked at the blood.

"You bit me," he said in disbelief.

He charged me and we rolled and tumbled, biting, scratching and pounding on each other. Ribs cracked and bones broke. Cinnamon yelled for us to stop but we were beyond words. I got on top of him and pinned him, pummeling him with a thunderstorm of paw strikes. He slid out from under me and rumbled into the trees.

"Okay, Cinnamon," I said, turning toward her, but she was gone. I saw the blur of her behind as she raced across the mudflats.

"MR. BROWN, ARE YOU OKAY?"

"I've lost my sense of smell."

"That can be a challenge for us bears."

"Yes, a challenge to go along with my 40 puncture wounds, a wide hole in my chest, broken ribs, a broken nose, a dislocated shoulder and a cracked skull."

"Tell me about it."

"I slipped on a salmon carcass."

"Uh-huh."

We sat in silence. I waited for her to ask me a question. Finally I spoke.

"Mating is overrated."

"What aspect of mating do you find overrated?" Dr. Chordata asked.

"All of it."

"I wonder how you arrived at that conclusion."

I shot the doctor a dirty look and raked the ground with my claws.

"Mr. Brown, do you want to talk about what happened to you? This is a small valley. I know about your fight with another bear over Cinnamon. Stop at any salmon stream or berry patch and one can hear all the gory details."

I stood up and roared. "If I hadn't listened to you I wouldn't have this problem!"

I quickly dug a three-foot-deep hole and sat in it. Dr. Chordata paused and exhaled a deep flow of breath.

"Believe me, Mr. Brown, blaming bears for

your bad behavior is not the answer to your problem. The blame for your bad behavior rests on your shoulder blades. We bears are not angry by nature. That's an anti-Ursinic myth that humans have used against bears for years as an excuse to murder us and you're basically buying into that b.s."

I stood up from my hole and paced.

"Let's talk about choices."

"Okay," I said, ripping an elderberry bush from the ground. "Here's a choice for you. I'm choosing to leave the Chilkat Valley."

"Where are you going?"

"I don't know. Somewhere in the Lower 48, like Colorado or California, where a bear can get a fair shake."

"And you think going there will make a difference?"

"Nothing I do here makes a difference."

"Moving to another range won't resolve a bear's issues."

I stopped pacing and turned to Dr. Chordata. "Wasting my time with you week after week hasn't resolved any issues, either."

As I stormed from Dr. Chordata's office I fell into the hole I had dug. I jumped out and stomped through the brush. I heard her voice behind me.

"Good luck, Mr. Brown, be careful of falling into the holes you dig."

I LIMPED ALONG ABOVE THE TREE LINE, LOOKING down on the valley. Good riddance, I thought. I couldn't wait to get away from the negativity of my old range. California, here I come! I'd heard the humans in California loved brown bears so much they put an image of us on their state flag. I saw myself sitting by a pristine river with a sweet sow feeding me berries as I dipped my feet in a cool stream on a hot summer day.

Pain sliced into my injured shoulders as I moved downhill toward the river. My left fore leg gave out on me and I tumbled end over end. I hit a tree, bounced off a stump, smashed into another tree, rolled through a thicket of Devil's Club, the plants thorns ripping at my fur. I knew a cliff edge was near but I couldn't slow my momentum.

There was a brief euphoric flash when I fell off the edge, a feeling of weightlessness and peace and freedom, before I dropped like a boulder. I let out a painful roar as I landed on a car parked on the side of the road. I lay there, the violence of the impact echoing through my body. I tentatively flexed my muscles, checking for new injuries.

I heard high pitched whimpers, like a coyote's, and I hoped it wasn't me. The sound came from inside the car and I lowered my head to look inside. Two humans, a male and a female, were curled up together in the back of the car. When they saw me they screamed. I'd never seen humans without their coats on.

It wasn't pretty.

I slid off the car and dragged my body across the road to the river. The chill in the air told me the glaciers had slowed their melting, lowering the level of the rivers, but without my sense of smell I had no sense of direction. Walking along the mudflats, disoriented, I understood for the first time what it was like to be lost. When I reached an island full of cottonwoods, the crushing weight of ten years of little sleep and bad dreams and lost hope landed on me like an old-growth spruce tree. I passed out.

I WATCH MYSELF AS I AM WHEELED, APPARENTLY unconscious, into the emergency room of the Cedar-Spruce-Hemlock Medical Center. A black bear wearing a jacket with "BEARMEDIC" on the back pushes me toward Triage.

"This bear needs immediate attention!" the bearmedic yells.

A bored brown bear nurse, chewing on a bone, tosses paperwork on the desk.

*"Fill out his managed bear care informa-
tion and have a seat."*

*The bearmedic leans in close on the
nurse.*

"This bear is going into hibernation!"

*The nurse drops her bone and rushes
from behind the desk.*

"Why didn't you say so?"

*The bearmedic and the nurse wheel me
through swinging doors and down a hallway full of bear doctors and nurses.*

*"Code Brown, bears! Code Brown!" the
nurse screams.*

*I am surrounded by a surgical team as
shiny instruments are passed back and
forth. The head surgeon holds his paws up
in front of him while an assistant files his
claws to a sharp, gleaming edge.*

"Nurse, how's the patient?"

*"Pulse is at eight, down from forty beats
per minute; temperature is ninety, down*

from 110; respiratory rate is two, down from ten breaths per minute."

The head surgeon nods grimly. He looks around.

"He's hibernating, all right. Where's the DeHibernation Unit?"

A Brown Bear Brass Band struts into the operating room and circles the bed. I have a tuba in one ear, a trombone in the other and trumpets in my face. The head surgeon lays his razor sharp claws on my stomach.

"On three...one...two...three!"

The band blasts its music at me and the surgeon tickles me with his claws. I leap up, eyes wide open, holding my paws to my ears.

"I'm tired of this! I want to go to sleep!" I yell at the doctor.

The doctor, still tickling me, removes his surgical mask. It is Dr. Chordata, who shakes her head at me.

"Good boy bears can't go to sleep until they clean up their dens and yours is a mess from all the holes you've dug."

"I want to go to sleep!" I yell again as the drummer from the band clashes his cymbals in my ear.

"TAKE NAPS NOW YOU WON'T BE ABLE TO SLEEP ALL winter."

I woke up, a voice from long ago beating on my eardrums. I was face down in the mud, my nose, ears and mouth full of glacial silt from the river. I shook my head and an avalanche of pain rumbled through my throbbing skull. I sniffed the air, hoping for a connection to the world. Still nothing.

"You lay around in the river bed you'll

catch your death of pneumonia."

My body freezes, my stomach tightens.

"But you won't have to worry about that if you don't start eating," the cracking voice continued. "A bear loses fifteen to forty percent of its body weight over the winter. You know that. And watch what you eat. Stay away from that fast food road kill. Full of parasites."

Was I still dreaming? I tested my level of consciousness by pounding my head against the ground. Numbing pain flashed through my body.

"Once upon a time a young bear didn't eat enough for the winter. Wouldn't listen to his mother no matter how many times she told him to eat and eat and eat. He was so thin when he crawled out of his den in the spring an eagle swooped down and carried him off. The eagle tore the meat right off the little bear's bones. Then the eagle lined his nest with the little bear's coat. True story. Should have listened to his mother."

I stumbled to my feet, my legs unsteady. I turned toward the voice. An old sow stood facing me on all fours in the low bushes. Her coat had the dull, grayish blue of the ground cover going to seed on the mountains. Patches of fur were missing, exposing sores on her body.

"I was walking a mile or so upwind of here when I caught a whiff of you and I thought I better check up on how you were doing."

"I'm fine," I said, groaning as I inhaled, my lungs expanding into my cracked ribs. I scratched at the river bed.

"Sure doesn't look like it to me. What are you doing? You're making a mess."

I looked down at the hole I was digging.

"I'm digging."

"Yes, I can tell that. You were always a digger, just like your father."

"What about my father?"

"Oh, please," my mother said, dismissing my question with a wave of her paw. "What a loser. Last I heard he was in the Alaskan Fish and Game Relocation Program. Classic garbageholic. We live in a valley with five types of salmon, three different trout, seventeen kinds of berries and some of the biggest moose in the world. So what does your father do? Spends his days and nights with those other deadbeat dads down at the garbage dump eating human trash. Human food will give you tumors the size of a porcupine's butt."

"You told us baby-eating monsters lived in the garbage dumps," I said, memories flickering in my head.

"And when was the last time you were at the dump?"

"Never," I said.

"It worked, didn't it?"

My mother contorted her round face and limped at me with her paws extended. "I smell the scent of a brown bear cub," she snarled, swiping at me with her claws.

"That's not funny," I said as I felt a smile bubbling up from deep inside me.

My mother sat down beside me and brushed gravel and silt off my face.

"I didn't want you to grow up and be a garbage bear like your father. I knew how hard headed male bears can be so I felt I had to scare you to prepare you for the world."

"Well," I said, the tension in my body softening.

"Now, you're not hard headed are you?" my mother said.

I looked down in the water, feeling young and embarrassed.

"Look," my mother said, pointing toward the sinking sun.

We sat together quietly and watched the

salmon colored sky slowly darken. As the last rays of light flickered away I fell asleep on my mother's shoulder.

I am at the Fall Sale at Bed, Bear and Behind, a popular store in the valley. A young human female with blond hair, about the size of a coyote, greets me. I am surprised when she speaks to me in fluent Bear and offers me complimentary porridge.

"No, thank you," I say, "Porridge is never just right for me. It's always too hot or too cold."

We walk over to the bed section.

"These beds have all been slept in," she tells me.

"Obviously," I say.

"Oh, my," she says, pointing to a small bed, "look at this Baby Bear bed. Not too soft, not too hard. It's what I use."

"I'm not a baby bear," I say, reeling from her human odor and moving down wind of her.

"Oh, my, this is the Mama Bear bed, very soft."

"No thanks, I'm not a Mama Bear."

"Oh, my, this is the Papa Bear bed. It can be very hard and difficult to sleep in."

"Let's see."

I crawl into the bed and curl up.

"This bed is exactly what I've been look-ing for," I say to the little blonde-haired human. "This isn't as hard as it looks. I'll take it."

I WOKE UP AND MY MOTHER WAS GONE. IT WAS morning and soft raindrops pressed on me like squirrel's feet. I stood up and my nose filled with the life of the valley. Yes, my smell was back! I sucked on the sweet scent of the high bush cranberry. The musty smell of decomposing leaves made me dizzy.

I spent the next few weeks eating salmon and berries, putting on 10 pounds a day. My beat up body needed plenty of healing so I decided to turn in early for the winter. Next year would be a good year for me, I said to myself as I walked across the valley. I found a well worn trail and headed up the mountain to dig my den. Walking through a densely covered section of the forest I smelled humans up ahead. I slipped behind a stand of alders to avoid scaring them. When the humans were safely down wind I stood up and let out a powerful roar. I wanted all the creatures out there to know the news.

Who's the bear? I'm the bear!

PRAISE FOR OTHER STORIES BY TOM LANG

Coffee

"…a deliciously satirical tale…"

   –*The Oregonian*

"A 'Days of Java and Roses' parody…59 hilarious pages."

   –*Willamette Week*

cat

"Tom Lang's **cat** offers a deceptively deep and complex story in the guise of a simple tale about a reformed cat hater and his feline, Bouhaki. Lang paints his characters with deft strokes, sweetly hooking his unsuspecting reader's heart."

   –Shannon Brownlee, Senior Editor, *U.S. News & World Report*

eagle

"Absolutely hilarious! Lang has created a unique and clever look at eagles."

   –Alaska Raptor Rehabilitation Center

BOUDELANG PRESS ORDER FORM

NAME_____

STREET_____

CITY_____STATE_____ZIP_____

Add $1 for shipping on individual book orders. For 3 or more books, add a flat $3.

	mrs. claus		TOTAL
Quantity	_____	x $7=	_____
Coffee	cat	eagle	
_____	_____	_____	x $5=	_____
salmon	bear		
_____	_____	x $5=	_____
Shipping		+	_____

TOTAL DUE = _____

__ **MASTERCARD** __ **VISA** __ **CHECK**

CARD #_____

EXP. DATE_____

PRINT NAME AS SHOWN ON CARD

_____

Please make checks payable to:

BOUDELANG PRESS

P.O Box 3005, Venice, CA 90291-9998

Questions? Please call 310.712.5606 or e-mail us at BOUDELANG@aol.com. Please visit our website www.boudelang.com.